W9-DEK-555

07/2011

An I Can Read Book™

Emma's YUCKY BROTHER

story by Jean Little

pictures by Jennifer Plecas

HarperTrophy®
An Imprint of HarperCollinsPublishers

This story is for Jane Glaves and Lorna and Doug Massey,
who are three of the world's best foster parents.
—J.L.

For Emma and Ante
—J.P.

HarperCollins®, 📖®, Harper Trophy®, and I Can Read Book®
are trademarks of HarperCollins Publishers Inc.

Emma's Yucky Brother
Text copyright © 2001 by Jean Little
Illustrations copyright © 2001 by Jennifer Plecas
Manufactured in China. All rights reserved.
www.harperchildrens.com

Library of Congress Cataloging-in-Publication Data
Little, Jean.
  Emma's yucky brother / story by Jean Little ; pictures by Jennifer Plecas.
    p.   cm. — (An I can read book)
  Summary: Emma finds out how hard it is to be a big sister when her family adopts a
four-year-old boy named Max.
  ISBN 0-06-028348-3 — ISBN 0-06-028349-1 (lib. bdg.) — ISBN 0-06-444258-6 (pbk.)
  [1. Brothers and sisters—Fiction. 2. Adoption—Fiction.] I. Plecas, Jennifer, ill.
II. Title. III. Series.
PZ7.L7225Ey   2000   99-34515
[Fic]—dc21   CIP
                                                                          AC

First Harper Trophy Edition, 2002
❖

CONTENTS

Emma's Big News

Emma Frost ran next door

to her best friend's house.

"Sally, guess what," she yelled.

"My brother is coming tomorrow!"

"Great!" Sally yelled back.

Sally's brother, Josh, shook his head.

"You don't have a brother," he said.

"We are adopting one," said Emma.

"He's four, and his name is Max.

Look, here's his picture."

The picture showed Max

playing with a toy car.

"What a great car!" Josh said.

"I got it for him with my own money,"
said Emma, "and Mom took it to him.
I can't wait to meet Max!"

"He will be a pest," said Sally.

"All brothers are pests."

"Not me," said Josh. "I'm great."

"My brother will be great, too,"

said Emma.

"He will be little and sweet.

And he's coming to visit tomorrow!"

"Brothers don't visit,"

Josh said. "Brothers stay."

"Adopted brothers visit first,"

said Emma. "When they are ready,

they stay. Before we could adopt Max,

we had to meet Miss Day.

She helps people adopt kids.

She had to visit our house

and check us out.

Then she told us about Max,

and Mom and Dad got to meet him.

Now it's my turn."

"You've waited forever," said Sally.

"Max is worth it," Emma said.

"Having a brother will be great!"

"Maybe," said Sally.

"Brothers are great sometimes.

But brothers are pests, too."

"You will see, Sally," said Emma.

"Max will be the best brother ever!"

Max's Visit

Emma and Mom made cookies.

Miss Day came over with Max.

"Hi, Emma," Miss Day said.

"Max loves the car you sent him."

Emma stared at Max.

15

In the picture, he had looked little.

But this boy was big.

He did not smile at her.

Emma got the cookies.

"We made yummy cookies

for you, Max," she said.

Max grabbed four.

He ate them all very fast.

"They are not yummy," he said.

"They are yucky, yucky, YUCKY!"

The grown-ups sat and talked.

Max played with his car.

"I got you that," Emma said.

Max put the car down.

"No you didn't," he said.

Sally came over.

"Is Max little and sweet?" she asked.

"No," said Emma.

"He called my cookies yucky."

"That's nothing," Sally said.

"Josh calls me Yucky Sally."

"Come meet him," said Emma.

"Hi, Max," Sally said.

"I'm Sally Gray from next door.

My brother, Josh, is four like you.

Do you want to meet him?"

Max took Sally's hand.

"Okay," he said.

"Let's play tag," Max said.

"You're it, Yucky Sally," said Josh.

"Chase me, Sally!" Max yelled.

"I will chase you," said Emma.

"No, not you," Max said.

"I want Sally to chase me!"

Later, Miss Day came out.

"Time to go, Max," she said.

"No way, Miss Day," said Max.

"I want to stay

with Josh and Sally."

"Race you to the car, Max,"

Sally said. "One, two, three, GO!"

Max won.

"Get in and wave," Sally said.

"Then we can wave back to you."

Max waved and waved.

"Good-bye, Sally," he shouted.

Emma ran inside.

"I don't like Max," Emma said.

"He isn't little.

He isn't sweet.

He hates my cookies,

and he likes Sally best."

26

"Sally has Josh," Dad said.

"She knows about brothers
and will help you with Max."

"I don't need Sally," Emma yelled,

"and I don't need a brother.

Brothers are nothing but pests!"

Their Boy

A week later, Max came back.

"Where is Sally?" he asked.

"Sally is not your sister.

I am," said Emma.

"No way, Yucky Emma," Max said.

Josh came over to play.

Josh and Max played tag,

and Max fell down.

Mom got a Band-Aid for Max.

"I want Jane," Max cried.

Jane was Max's foster mother.

Later, Emma asked,

"Why doesn't Jane adopt Max?"

"Jane's home is special," Mom said.

"Kids who need a new home stay there

until they are adopted.

They need Jane's love and care.

But she can't adopt so many, Emma."

The next time Max came,

he stayed all night.

At bedtime he cried for Jane again.

Dad took Max on his lap and said,

"Missing people is hard.

I know because I miss you

when you are at Jane's."

"Me too," said Mom.

"We want you to stay with us

and be our boy," said Dad.

"How about it, Max?"

Max held on to Dad.

The Frosts waited.

"Maybe I will be your boy,"

Max said.

Dad hugged Max tight.

"That's great, just great," Dad said.

"Will you be my dad?" Max asked.

"Or will you still be Emma's dad?"

"I will always be Emma's dad,

but I want to be your dad, too,"

Dad said.

Emma got on Mom's lap.

Mom hugged her tight.

"I love you, Emma," she said.

"Do you love me, too?"

Max asked.

"Yes, you, too," Mom said.

Max fell asleep on Dad's lap.

He looked little and sweet.

Emma smiled at him.

"Max sure is a pest," she said,

"but he is the best pest ever."

Max Comes to Stay

Soon Max came to visit

for a whole weekend.

Then at last

he came to stay for good.

Miss Day did not come in

with him this time.

Max stood by the door

and held his fast car tight.

"Come on in, Max," said Mom.

Max stayed where he was.

He looked very little.

Emma got some cookies

and bit into a big one.

"Yummy, yummy," she said.

Max ran behind her chair.

His hand came out.

Emma handed him a cookie.

"More," Max said.

"Pig," said Emma.

"Don't call Max a pig," Mom said.

"He's your little brother, Emma."

"I'm not little. I'm BIG," Max yelled.

Emma handed Max another cookie.

"Say, 'Thank you, sister,'" she said.

Max ran up the stairs.

"Yucky Emma!" he yelled.

"I don't need a sister!

Sisters are yucky!"

41

"Dad, Max hates me," Emma said.

"Make him stop calling me

Yucky Emma."

"Let it go, Emma," Dad said.

"Max isn't used to us yet.

This is hard for him."

"It's hard for me, too!"

Emma shouted.

"Yes, it is," Dad said,

"but soon it will be easier

for both of you."

"Supper time," said Mom.

"Please go get Max, Emma,"

said Dad.

Max was under his bed.

"Come and eat, Max," Emma said.

"Eat what?" asked Max.

"Hot dogs," Emma told him.

Max came out slowly.

Emma saw tears on his face.

She held out her hand to him.

Max took it and held on tight.

They went downstairs together.

Max's Sister

One day Emma and Sally were playing.

"You said brothers are pests,"

said Emma. "You were right."

"I think Max is great," Sally said,

"and so do you, Emma Frost."

47

"Well, sometimes," Emma said,

"but not when he calls me

Yucky Emma."

Just then Max's car

shot into the room

and under Emma's bed.

"Max Frost, get lost!" Emma yelled.

"I need my fast car," Max said.

He went under the bed.

The bed jumped and bumped.

Emma's doll Grace fell.

Jump, bump, thump! went the bed.

Max came out

with Grace and his car.

"Sally, can I play, too?" he asked.

"Sally's playing with me,"

Emma said, "so get lost, Max."

"You can't make me," Max said.

"Let's lose *him*, Sally," Emma said.

The girls ran away.

Later, Emma and Sally found Grace.

Her head was off.

Max's car was there,

but Max was not.

"I'm telling Mom," Emma said.

Sally said, "Don't tell, Emma.

You can fix her."

Emma snapped on Grace's head.

Then Emma picked up Max's car.

"He always takes this," she said.

"Where do you think he is?"

"When Josh breaks things,

he runs away," Sally said.

"Maybe Max does that, too."

"Max!" Emma called.

Max did not answer.

The girls looked everywhere,

but they did not find Max.

"Mom, Max ran away,"

Emma said. "I told him to get lost,

and he did."

"We will find him," Mom said.

But they didn't.

They looked all over the house.

They looked in the yard,

and down the street.

It was time for supper.

Nobody was hungry.

It was time for Sally to go home.

She stayed.

Emma was crying.

"He is a pest," she said,

"but he is my brother."

Emma ran back outside alone.

"Max, where are you?" she called.

"Please say something!"

"Something," said a big bush.

Emma jumped.

Then she laughed.

"Come out, Max," she said.

A dirty little boy came out.

His face was wet with tears.

Emma hugged him, dirt and all.

"Boy, am I glad you're here,"

Emma said.

Max looked away.

"Did you find Grace?" he asked.

"I tried to fix her, Emma,

but I couldn't."

"I fixed her," Emma said.

"But don't run away again, Max.

Next time, ask me for help.

That's what sisters are for."

Mom and Dad hugged them.

Sally said, "Good for Yucky Emma!"

"Don't call her that," Max said.

"Emma isn't yucky.

She's my sister."